For my hot air balloons: Noah, Milo, Zen and Lotus

www.theenglishschoolhouse.com

ISBN: 978-1-955130-07-3

GENEVIEVE AND THE GIANT

BY DR. TAMARA PIZZOLI ILLUSTRATED BY ELENA TOMMASI FERRONI

Gillian the giant came from a long line of BIG people.
Not only were the giants in her family enormous in size,
they were also known the world over for being remarkably
successful in business.

Gillian was the youngest of generations of giants.
Her great-grandfather, Geoffrey Ludwig Giant, had willed
his entire estate to her, and at a very young age
Gillian became the owner of a substantial amount of land.

She'd been listed in Giants magazine as one of the
wealthiest giants in the world.

Things were easy enough for Gillian while she was young, but when she became an adult at age eighteen, the real responsibilities came.

Every city and all of the households that were willed to her by her great-uncle were now her responsibility.

Though she was young, Gillian began managing the duties of a landlord on a very large scale.
She collected rent and taxes from thousands and thousands of people, and if she wasn't paid on time, Gillian did the unpleasant work of evicting her tenants, which is just another way of saying kicking people out of her properties.

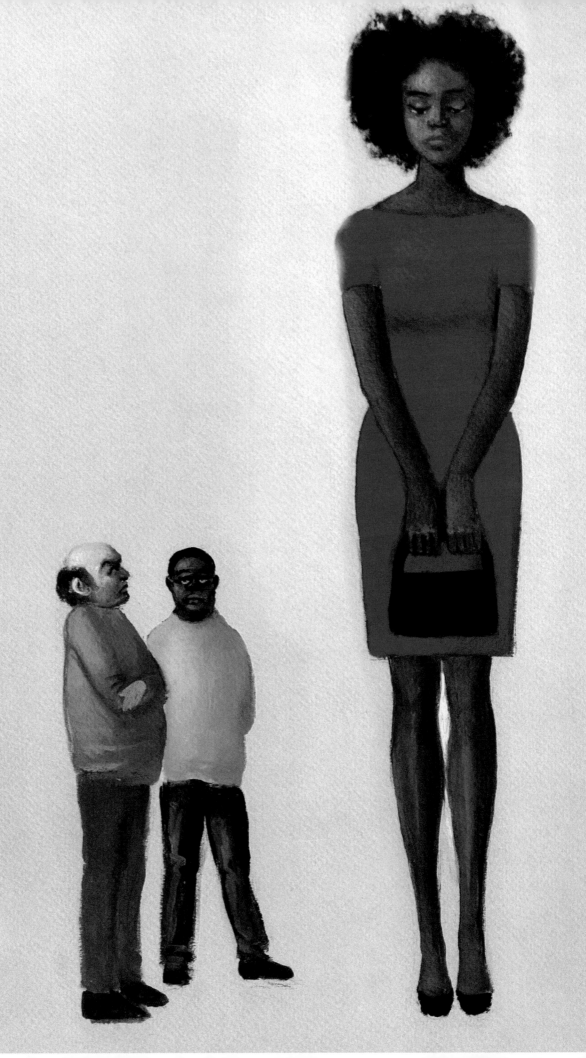

Though Gillian considered herself to be a regular,
down-to-earth person, the people who paid her disagreed.

She received plenty of complaints, stares, dirty looks, eye rolls,
and snide remarks.

Gillian found it difficult to do day-to-day activities with ease.

Eventually the negativity grew to be too much for Gillian. She owned all she could ever want on the earth anyway, so Gillian decided to pack up her belongings and move her big, beautiful self to the sky.

It's easy enough to do,
if you can afford the relocation.
And Gillian could.

Once settled, Gillian only had to figure out the details.
She hired a team of accountants and managers to
handle her business on the ground, and Gillian arranged
to have all other necessities shipped to her new house
she had built in the clouds.

And because the giant lifestyle, or living large, requires tons of maintenance, hot air balloons carrying both services and servants departed from the ground headed to Gillian's sky mansion daily.

Once Gillian settled in her new home, she stayed there.
Years passed and she never stepped foot on the ground again.

The fact she wasn't around anymore didn't stop the people who lived below her from talking about Gillian one bit, and as the years passed, Gillian the giant had quite the reputation.

There were some who called her difficult, and others who insisted she was cruel. In her absence, Gillian was blamed for things that weren't even her fault or concern.

When it rained, some people said it was because
Gillian was either crying or flushing her toilet.

Every day after school, Genevieve Gibson watched
the hot air balloons ascend into the clouds from her
family's antique stand at the local outdoor market.
She too longed to go up into the sky.

The fare for each hot air balloon ride was thirty
dollars, a price far to steep for her to pay.

Then, one Wednesday evening just around dusk, Genevieve made a decision. She stuffed a valuable antique hourglass from her family's stand into her pocket, and while her mother and grandmother closed down their shop, Genevieve rushed over to the nearest sky taxi and thrust the hourglass toward the man selling rides. "Here!" she panted, "I want to meet the giant."
But before the man could answer, a wrinkly, cold hand clasped Genevieve by the wrist and squeezed tightly.

"Girl, where are you going?" a shrill voice began.
Genevieve turned and noticed the hand holding her belonged to an old woman she'd never seen before.
"You can't just go flying off in a hot air balloon with some stranger!" the elderly lady scolded.

Genevieve nodded,
as she knew what the
woman had just said was the
truth. She turned to retrieve
the hourglass, but the sky taxi
was already meters up in the clouds.
The man had left, with one of her family's most valuable pieces
to sell in tow. Tears began to stream down Genevieve's cheeks.

"Now, now sweet pea," the old woman began,
"Don't you cry. All is not lost." The elderly woman pulled a small
ivy plant from her coat pocket. She looked Genevieve in the
eyes and said, "Run right home. Plant this outside your front
door. Then wait until tomorrow morning."

Genevieve had many questions, but before she could ask even
one, the old woman pivoted and disappeared into the crowd.

Genevieve wiped her face and headed home.
Once she arrived, she did just as the old lady instructed
and planted the tiny ivy plant in her family's front yard.

Much to Genevieve's surprise, the next morning the entire
house was covered in ivy, and a stalk of the plant stretched
from the chimney clear to the sky.

For Genevieve, there was only one thing to do, really.
She began to climb.

It took all morning and most of the afternoon for her to reach her destination. When she was at the very tip of the last ivy leaf, Genevieve leapt off and found herself at the entrance of what she knew was Gillian the giant's palace.

"I've seen pictures of this in my history book."
Genevieve said to herself as the door to the giant's home opened on its own.

Upon entering, Genevieve stood with her mouth wide open. She'd never laid eyes on such opulence and splendor. She scurried like a mouse down the longest hallway she'd ever seen, and hid behind a large pillar.

After some time, a voice startled her.

"Did you come here to just stand around
or do you plan on earning your day's pay?"
a deep voice said.

Genevieve turned and was surprised to see the man
from the hot air balloon the day before waving a
spoon as big as she was at her.

"Put this apron on and follow me. Gillian can't stand
for her breakfast to be late."
As soon as the man had uttered those words, a
powerful voice boomed from the dining room:

"FEE FI FO FUM! Y'ALL BRING MY GRITS AND
SOME CINNAMON BUNS."

Genevieve stood speechless. "You heard the woman!"
the man from the hot air balloon said in a huff.

Soon the hallway was swarming with people—
a few Gillian recognized from the market square.
Everyone made their way to the dining hall.

Genevieve couldn't believe the spread that was right before her very eyes, and just how many people it took to feed the giant. There was a lot of heavy lifting involved. Genevieve was given the task of delivering the giant's spoon. As she dragged the golden utensil over to the giant's linen napkin, Gillian stopped her with her fingertip.

"You're new," the giant began as she peered at Genevieve.
"What's your name?"
"Genevieve, Ms. Gillian," she began.
"My name is Genevieve. It's nice to meet you."
The giant picked the girl up and placed her on her spoon.
She lifted her close, leaned over, and squinted her eyes.
"Why aren't you in school today?"
"I...I..." Genevieve began, "I just wanted to come work for a day, and help my mom and grandma out. We could use extra money....and....um...just...please don't eat me."

The entire room erupted in laughter. The giant laughed loudest.
"Eat you?!" she scoffed, "Baby girl, why would I do such a thing?"
"She got grits!" the man from the hot air balloon chuckled.

The rest of the day, Genevieve hung out with Gillian.
The pair talked about everything and nothing,
and Genevieve explained to the giant that she'd heard
terrible things about her practically her whole life.
Genevieve explained, "They say you're mean and awful,
and that people get up here and never come back.
They say when it rains it's because you're flushing the
toilet."

Gillian smiled and replied, "You know what they say,
baby girl, believe none of what you hear and half of
what you see. I've been trying to get tons of these
folks up in here to go home for years, but they say
they like it better in the sky."

As night fell, Genevieve sat and gazed at the most
spectacular view of the moon. Gillian joined her.
She quietly counted out a thousand dollars in one
hundred dollar bills, and placed the payment in
Genevieve's hand for her day's work... and for the
pleasant conversation. Genevieve couldn't believe her
eyes or her luck.

"This is enough for my mama to pay rent!"
she exclaimed as she thanked the giant.
"I don't wanna go home," Genevieve began, but my
mom and grandma will start to worry about me."

"I'll walk with you," the giant smiled.
The trip proved to be much quicker on the giant's
shoulders.

But when Genevieve and the giant reached the ground,
an unexpected welcome awaited.
"Give me my daughter!" Genevieve's mother demanded.
The rest of the townspeople shouted angrily at the
giant, accusing her of all sorts of wrongdoing.

Genevieve looked toward Gillian,
and noticed that her shoulders were softly shaking.
Her lower lip was trembling. Her eyes began to water,
and just as the first tear fell, the entire sky opened,
and rain began to fall. Genevieve cleared her throat
and screamed at the crowd.

"I spent the whole day at Gillian the giant's house!
She was kind and generous and friendly! She paid me
very well for a day's work."

Genevieve took the wad of cash out and the crowd
gasped. Genevieve's grandmother came and shooed
her granddaughter into the house as she scolded,
"Now baby how many times do I got to tell you,
you can't just go around showing folks how much
money you've got!"

Gillian the giant spoke, "I know many of you do not like me," she began. "But I am here and I am listening."

The crowd of townspeople that had gathered made their complaints known to Gillian the giant.

And she listened, just as she said she would.
And from that day on, Gillian the giant found herself spending more time down on the ground, and the people of the land spent considerably more time in the sky.

Made in the USA
Columbia, SC
11 November 2021

48755310R00022